JALANI AND THE LOCK

LORENZO PACE

The Rosen Publishing Group's

PowerKids Press

New York

This book is dedicated to the oldest living member of the Pace family, my dear Uncle Julius Pace, who presented the original lock to me and to my mother, Mary Alice Pace (1916–1993), and father, Bishop Elder Eddie T. Pace (1909–1991). The book is also dedicated to my children: Shawn, Ezra, Jalani, for whom the main character is named, and my daughter Esperanza; and to my favorite Uncle Bill and Aunt Evelyn Clark and my Aunt Elnora (Pewee) Baker, in Birmingham, Alabama.

With special thanks to Khadda Madani, my fabulous assistant editor and director of the Open Door Fashion and Art Gallery in New York City; to my great friend and colleague Dr. Geoffrey Newman, dean of the School of the Arts, Montclair State University, Montclair, New Jersey; to Chanel Cook, my homegirl and personal attorney; to Curtis Cook and Mildred Cook, who is director of curriculum and testing for the Orange Board of Education, Orange, New Jersey; and a very special thanks to my high school chum Dr. Raymond Dalton, Executive Director of Minority Affairs, Cornell University, Ithaca, NY, who had encouraged me from day one to go back to school and to keep making art; and to my old ChiTown buddy and entrepreneur Walter Patrick without his suggestion to the club publisher this book may not have happened; to my dear brother, Seneca Turner, a poet, philosopher, and great warrior; to my friend and master painter Joe Overstreet and Corinne Jennings of Kenkeleba Galleries of New York City who together have built a great art institution and have shown my artwork in their galleries for many years; to Roger Rosen, who had the courage and vision to make this book a reality; and to all my brothers—Eddie, Lawrence, Michael, Alfonzo, William, and Ronald— and sisters—Dorothy, Mary, Roslyn, and Shirley; and lastly, to my nieces, nephews, and cousins in the Pace family.

Thanks to all the visionaries who believe in the essence of humanity—that we can all live in peace and harmony.

Published in 2001 by The Rosen Publishing Group, Inc.
29 East 21st Street, New York, NY 10010

First Edition

Book Design: Kim Sonsky

Illustrator: Lorenzo Pace

Pace, Lorenzo.
Jalani and the Lock / by Lorenzo Pace.
– 1st ed.
        p. cm.
Summary: In this story based on true events, Jalani, a freed slave, gives the lock that held him in chains to his eldest child as a symbol of his enslavement. Includes information about African Burial Ground Memorial Sculpture in New York City created by Jalani's descendent, Lorenzo Pace.
    ISBN 0-8239-9700-6
    (lib. bdg.)
    [1. Slavery—Fiction. 2. Afro-Americans—Fiction.] I. Title.
    PZ7.P117 Jal 2001
    [E]—dc21

                                                              00-009274

Manufactured in the United States of America

JALANI
AND
THE
LOCK

A long time ago in Africa

4

a little boy named Jalani

loved to play in the forest.

The forest was very beautiful to Jalani.
Everywhere he looked
there was life and magic.

Jalani's mother told him many times
not to play in the forest by himself,
but he played there anyway.

One day, when Jalani was playing in the forest with his imaginary friends,

a strange man came and took him away

on a big boat with hundreds of other people

to a far-off land.

Locks

and chains were put on Jalani.

24

He was forced to work all day with very little food and was never allowed to play again.

Jalani was forced to change many things:
his name, his clothes, his food,
and even his language.

JALANi

But they could not change his memories of home.

Many years passed and Jalani had almost given up
all hope of ever being free.

One day a tall man in a big black hat said that all slaves should be free.

And freedom finally came.

And Jalani was set free, but he kept the lock and key that had kept him in slavery.

Over the years, Jalani had lots
of children and grandchildren.

Just before he died, Jalani gave the lock to his eldest
son. He told his son that he must pass it on to his
own children one day,

so they would never forget from where they all came.

44

The lock pictured on the last page of this book originally shackled Steve Pace, the author and illustrator's great-great grandfather.

A bronze replica of the Pace family's original lock and key is interred within "Triumph of the Human Spirit," the African Burial Ground Memorial Sculpture created by Lorenzo Pace at Foley Square Park in New York City.

The sculpture is a tribute to the African burial ground rediscovered in 1991 during construction of a federal building north of Wall Street. This is the world's largest outdoor site-specific installation devoted to African Americans enslaved. A subsequent archaeological dig uncovered the remains of over 400 African New Yorkers as well as about 600 burial artifacts. The site is believed to have been in use from 1712 to 1794 and to have housed the remains of ten to twenty thousand. This site has been designated a National Historic Landmark.